This book belongs to:

Ant-tuition

Ant-tuition

David Kirk

CALLAWAY

NEW YORK

2008

Miss Spider and Squirt were busy preparing food to store for the winter.

"Can I go out and play, Mom?" Squirt begged. "Please?"

"Sorry, sweetie," Miss Spider replied. "We have to finish stashing our seeds. The first frost will be here before we know it!"

Struggling to carry a big basket of seeds, Squirt joined the other bugs as they filled the Hollow Stump in the meadow. While loading his seeds, Squirt stumbled. He rolled down a chute, fell into a cart, and bumped all the way down a hill, tumbling to a stop near the anthill.

"Woaaah!" he shouted.

"Hey, what's all the racket?" cried Ned and Ted.

"Sorry," Squirt said. "I've been working so hard, I lost my balance. Everybuggy is storing seeds to get ready for the first frost."

The ants dropped to the ground, rolling around and howling with laughter.

"Winter won't be coming anytime soon," chuckled Ned.

"How do you know?" Squirt wondered.

"Oh, it's just a hunch," Ted replied. "Call it our intuition."

"Or our 'ant'-tuition," laughed Ned.

"In fact," said Ted, "we're so sure that winter isn't coming that we're throwing a Summer's-Never-Ending party. Everybuggy's invited!"

Squirt surfed through Sunny Patch, spreading word of the party. Everybuggy cheered at the thought of all that fun!

"How do Ned and Ted know that summer's never ending?" asked Shimmer.

"They just know!" Squirt proclaimed. "It's their ant-tuition."

But Miss Spider wasn't so sure. "Hmmm . . . it's not smart to follow a hunch," she said.

Everybuggy in Sunny Patch dropped their work to go to the big party.

As all the kids buzzed out the door, Squirt asked his parents, "Why aren't you coming?"

"We have to finish filling the Hollow Stump," said Holley.

"Winter is on our doorstep," Miss Spider agreed. "We've seen the signs. Come along and we'll show you."

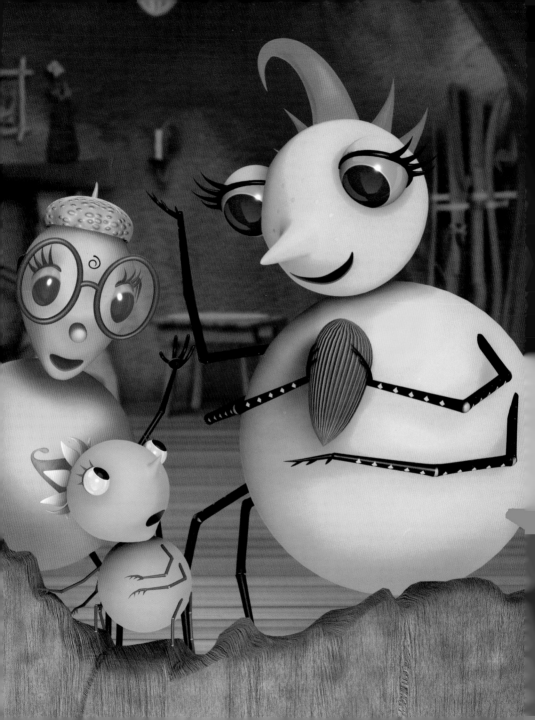

First, Miss Spider took Squirt to the Taddy Puddle. "Do you hear anything, Squirt?" she asked.

"No, it's so quiet. Hey, why aren't the frogs croaking?"

"All the frogs have burrowed in the mud for winter," Holley told him.

Just then, a flock of wild geese flew overhead, honking loudly.

"Look at those geese!" Squirt cried. "I wonder where they're going."

"They're flying south for the winter," Miss Spider explained, "where it's nice and warm."

"Because it's getting cold here," Squirt finished, nodding.

A cool breeze swirled the leaves.

"I guess Ned and Ted were wrong," Squirt shivered. "Winter *is* coming. Maybe we should get back to work and fill the Hollow Stump."

"Good idea!" Miss Spider and Holley agreed. They fetched the rest of the family from Ned and Ted's party and got back to work.

inally, after the rest of the food had been stored, Squirt and his family joined the ant brothers' party. All of a sudden, snow began to fall.

Everybuggy squealed in horror.

"Oh no! Winter's here after all!" cried Pillbug.

"We never finished storing seeds in the stump!" wailed Eunice.

"Don't worry," Squirt assured them, "our family finished filling the stump. There's plenty of food to last the entire winter."

After everybuggy had thanked them and gone home, Miss Spider's family heard sniffling coming from the anthill.

"We're going to be ant-sicles by morning, Ned," wept Ted.

"You poor ants had better come home with us," Miss Spider told them.

Back at the Cozy Hole, everybuggy's faces glowed in front of the warm and toasty fire.

"You know, Ned," said Ted. "It's really good to plan ahead."

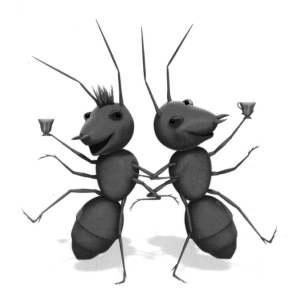

"I know, Ted," said Ned. "I have a hunch it's going to be a great winter."

Everybuggy laughed as they sipped hot cider.

This book is based on the TV episode "Ant-tuition," written by Nadine Van Der Velde,
from the animated TV series *Miss Spider's Sunny Patch Friends* on Nick Jr.,
a Nelvana Limited/Absolute Pictures Limited co-production in association
with Callaway Arts & Entertainment, based on the Miss Spider books by David Kirk.
Special thanks to the Nelvana staff, including Doug Murphy, Scott Dyer, Tracy Ewing, Pam Lehn,
Tonya Lindo, Mark Picard, Jane Sobol, Luis Lopez, Eric Pentz, and Georgina Robinson.

Library of Congress Cataloging-in-Publication Data is available.

ISBN 978-0-448-45026-1   10 9 8 7 6 5 4 3 2 1

ABOUT DAVID KIRK

Master artist and storyteller David Kirk is hailed as one of today's most innovative and exciting creators of books and toys for children. Before his remarkable success in the world of children's publishing, Kirk was the founder and designer of two toy companies. His bright, hand-painted wooden toys are, together with his paintings and hand-crafted furniture, treasured by collectors and featured in books, art galleries, and museums.

Then along came a spider: Miss Spider. Inspired by his daughter Violet's love for insects in the family garden, Kirk found the perfect subject for his story. *Miss Spider's Tea Party,* a lush counting book in verse with mesmerizing oil illustrations and an important message about tolerance, quickly became a phenomenon, earning praise from booksellers and librarians across the country. Kirk followed this success by continuing the saga of Miss Spider in *Miss Spider's Wedding, Miss Spider's New Car,* and *Miss Spider's ABC.*

In addition to creating splendid books and paintings, Mr. Kirk finds time to develop his many other projects, including designing Sunny Patch, a collection of children's lifestyle products, for Target stores. He is also executive producer of *Miss Spider's Sunny Patch Friends,* a 3-D computer-animated television series on Nick Jr. The success of the series inspired a line of trade and mass-market books published by Callaway Arts & Entertainment and Penguin Young Readers Group.

Mr. Kirk lives in upstate New York with his wife, Kathy, and daughters, Violet, Primrose, and Wisteria.